I LOVE
ZAYN
Are you his ultimate fan?

Written by Lauren Taylor

Edited by Bryony Jones
With thanks to Jonny Marx

Design by Barbara Ward
Cover design by Zoe Bradley

Picture Acknowledgements:
Front cover: Matt Baron/BEI/Rex Features
Back cover: Kevin Mazur/Getty Images

Picture section:
Page 1, Suzan/EMPICS Entertainment/Press Association Images
Page 2, Gilbert Carrasquillo/FilmMagic/Getty Images
Page 3, Al Pereira/WireImage/Getty Images
Page 4, Matt Baron/BEI/Rex Features
Page 5, Ken McKay/Rex Features
Pages 6–7, Kevin Winter/Getty Images
Page 8, KeystoneUSA-ZUMA/Rex Features

First published in Great Britain in 2013 by Buster Books,
an imprint of Michael O'Mara Books Limited, 9 Lion Yard, Tremadoc Road,
London SW4 7NQ

www.busterbooks.co.uk

Text copyright © Buster Books 2013

Artwork adapted from www.shutterstock.com

A CIP catalogue record for this book is available from the British Library.

ISBN: 978-1-78055-214-9

PLEASE NOTE: This book is not affiliated with or endorsed by One Direction or
any of their publishers or licensees.

10 9 8 7 6 5 4 3 2 1

Printed and bound in February 2013 by CPI Group (UK) Ltd, 108 Beddington Lane,
Croydon, CR0 4YY, United Kingdom.

Papers used by Buster Books are natural, recyclable products made from wood
grown in sustainable forests. The manufacturing processes conform to the
environmental regulations of the country of origin.

I LOVE
ZAYN
Are you his ultimate fan?

Buster Books

Contents

About this book   5

Forever young   6

Love by numbers   9

It's all in the stars   12

Super-fans   16

Favourite things   19

True or false?   22

What's your theme song? 24

What was the question?   26

Big hearts   28

Last first kiss   32

Sweet tweets   35

Diary dash   36

Let the dice decide   40

Guess who?   42

Twitterverse   45

Cringe!   46

The love calculator   48

Clowning around   49

Dream date   60

Would you rather?   62

Your perfect day   64

All directions!   68

So stylish   70

Star style   74

Dream big   76

Timeline   80

Read all about it!   84

Song scramble   86

Fact-tastic!   88

All the answers   91

About this book

When One Direction were famously voted out of hit-show *The X Factor* in the semi-finals, Zayn Malik uttered the prophetic words, 'This isn't the end of One Direction.' Well, he was right! Now the boys are an internatioal success and living in a whirlwind of fame.

Everyone has a favourite member of the band, and if yours is Zayn, then this is the book for you! It's crammed full of quizzes, facts, games and stories that will tell you everything you ever wanted to know about him.

What does Zayn look for in a girl? What's his signature style? What are his favourite things and what would you do on a date with him? Turn the page and find out all this and tons more. You'll soon be inZaynely expert on your favourite 1D star.

It's amaZayn!

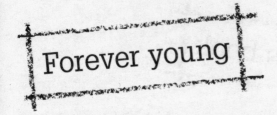

Forever young

HOW MUCH DO YOU KNOW ABOUT ZAYN'S LIFE BEFORE HE WAS FAMOUS? TAKE THIS QUIZ TO SEE IF YOU CAN OUTSHINE YOUR PALS WITH YOUR KNOWLEDGE OF ZAYN'S CHILDHOOD, THEN CHECK YOUR ANSWERS ON **PAGE 91**.

1. What were Zayn's favourite subjects at school?
  a. English and art
  b. French and cookery
  c. Chemistry and maths

2. What school musical did Zayn star in as a lad?
  a. *Bugsy Malone*
  b. *Oliver!*
  c. *Mary Poppins*

3. How old was Zayn when he was told by experts that he had a reading age of eighteen?
  a. Eight
  b. Nine
  c. Eleven

4. What was Zayn's first pet?

   a. A Staffordshire bull terrier called Tyson

   b. A Netherland dwarf rabbit called Nutmeg

   c. A Siamese cat called Twister

5. What is Zayn's earliest memory?

   a. Going to a fair with his mum and grandma

   b. Breaking his arm during a game of rounders

   c. Learning to swim at his local pool

6. What was Zayn's childhood hairstyling secret?

   a. Getting up half an hour early so his sister could do his hair

   b. Saving up all his pocket money for trips to an expensive salon

   c. Weekly conditioning treatments

7. What music was Zayn into as a kid?

   a. Punk and ska

   b. Classical guitar

   c. R&B and rap

8. How old was Zayn when he first had a girlfriend?

   a. Thirteen

   b. Seventeen

   c. Fifteen

9. How many cousins did Zayn grow up with?

   a. Five

   b. Eighteen

   c. Over twenty

10. What was the name of Zayn's nursery school?

   a. Cheeky Monkeys

   b. Little Sunshines

   c. He didn't go to nursery school – he stayed home with his dad.

11. What does Zayn say he was like as a child?

   a. 'I was very independent.'

   b. 'I spent all of my pocket money on sweets.'

   c. 'I used to ask the teachers for extra homework.'

12. Zayn has both European and Asian ancestry. Which of these describes his family's origin?

   a. Irish/English/Pakistani

   b. Scottish/English/Pakistani

   c. Welsh/English/Pakistani

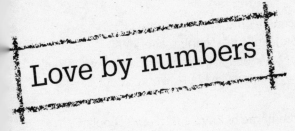

Love by numbers

ARE YOU AND ZAYN DESTINED TO LIVE
HAPPILY EVER AFTER? WELL, THAT ALL DEPENDS ON
YOUR 'LIFE NUMBER'. FOLLOW THE INSTRUCTIONS
BELOW TO CALCULATE YOUR COMPATIBILITY WITH YOUR
FAVOURITE 1D SUPERSTAR, AND DISCOVER WHICH 1D
SONG SUITS YOU BEST.

To find out your life number, add the digits of your birth
date together – the day, the month and the year.

For example, Zayn's birthday is 12th January 1993
(12/01/1993). To find out his life number, you would add:

$$1 + 2 + 0 + 1 + 1 + 9 + 9 + 3 = 26$$

Keep adding the totals together until you end up with just
one digit:

$$26 \text{ becomes: } 2 + 6 = 8$$

Zayn's life number is 8.

After you've worked out your own life number, check out
the following pages to find out how your compatibility
adds up.

Life number: 1
About you: Independent, determined, confident
1 and 8: Zayn loves confident girls. You're also both fiercely independent, so you'd never have to worry about having your own space.
Your song: 'Kiss You'

Life number: 2
About you: Peacekeeping, considerate, sensitive
2 and 8: Zayn would be lucky to have a girl like you to keep him smiling. But don't take it to heart when he spends weeks on the road.
Your song: 'First Last Kiss'

Life number: 3
About you: Friendly, adventurous, positive
3 and 8: Both you and Zayn love being centre stage. You'll have fun together, no matter what you do.
Your song: 'Live While We're Young'

Life number: 4
About you: Hard-working, helpful, practical
4 and 8: You and Zayn are both hard-working and like time spent at home. When he's not off on tour, he'll love coming home to you.
Your song: 'Gotta Be You'

Life number: 5
About you: Intelligent, fun-loving, free-spirited
5 and 8: Zayn finds intelligence especially attractive in

a girl. And with your easy-breezy nature, you'll have no trouble adjusting to Zayn's busy schedule.
Your song: 'One Thing'

Life number: 6
About you: Family-oriented, trustworthy, compassionate
6 and 8: Zayn loves his family, just like you. You'd both be very happy spending fun times with all your loved ones.
Your song: 'Little Things'

Life number: 7
About you: Sensitive, wise, reserved
7 and 8: As you and Zayn are both independent souls, you can be quite reserved. And as you're also both sensitive, you can read each other perfectly.
Your song: 'What Makes You Beautiful'

Life number: 8
About you: Organized, ambitious, a strong leader
8 and 8: There's no way you'd get on Zayn's nerves with your super-organized nature — you're just like him! You'll also totally inspire him with your ambition.
Your song: 'Up All Night'

Life number: 9
About you: multi-talented, emotional, determined
9 and 8: As an emotional soul, you'll probably fall in love with any song that Zayn writes. And as you're so multi-talented, maybe you can help out with any tough lyrics!
Your song: 'Heart Attack'

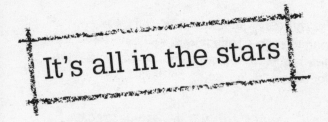

It's all in the stars

USE THIS ZAYN ZODIAC TO FIND OUT WHAT YOUR STAR
SIGN SAYS ABOUT YOU, AND DISCOVER HOW YOU COULD
FIT INTO ZAYN'S INNER CIRCLE.

★ ARIES (21st March – 20th April) ★

Energetic, competitive and sporty, you love adventure and
taking charge. No one would catch you playing a board
game or lying around watching TV – you just have to keep
on the move. You could be Zayn's:

Personal trainer

You're bursting with energy and love keeping fit. You'd
be great helping Zayn stay pumped and in shape for an
upcoming tour.

★ TAURUS (21st April – 21st May) ★

Your heart of gold means everyone should have someone
like you in their life. You are dependable and appreciate the
beautiful things in life. You could be Zayn's:

Best friend

You're loyal, reliable, a great listener and you have the
patience of a saint. What more could Zayn want in a
best friend?

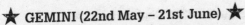

⭐ GEMINI (22nd May – 21st June) ⭐

You're known among your friends as a social butterfly. Fun to be around and full of sparkling conversation, you're the life and soul of the party. You could be Zayn's:

Party planner

You're confident, chatty and have no end of imagination for great party ideas. With your pizzazz and charm, you could make any event a hit, whether it's a sophisticated dinner party or an after-show bash.

⭐ CANCER (22nd June – 23rd July) ⭐

Your protective, caring and responsible nature means you are very good at looking after people. You also love to stay organized and take care of any outstanding business. You could be Zayn's:

Personal assistant

From organizing his schedule to protecting him from crazy fans, you would really take care of Zayn, and make him feel totally at ease.

⭐ LEO (24th July – 23rd August) ⭐

Dramatic and fun-loving, you like to be the centre of attention. You love shopping and have glamorous, show-stopping style, just like Zayn and his famous quiff. You could be Zayn's:

Date for the red carpet

You don't shy away from the spotlight, so that's why you would make the perfect partner for a swish showbiz bash. Slip on those heels and get ready to dress to impress.

★ VIRGO (24th August – 23rd September) ★

You are level-headed and precise, with a good memory. You're good at settling disputes and you won't stand for any laziness. You could be Zayn's:

Band manager

Life in One Direction is a roller-coaster ride. You'll have to book the best gigs for the band, while making sure the guys are happy. But if anyone can do it, you can!

★ LIBRA (24th September – 23rd October) ★

You love all things beautiful, and get a real thrill out of shopping! As you're also a thoughtful soul, you're always willing to help out your friends, too. You could be Zayn's:

Personal shopper

Zayn has to travel in style, but because of his busy schedule he doesn't always have the time to stay on top of the latest fashions. This is where you come in!

★ SCORPIO (24th October – 22nd November) ★

You are passionate and creative, and love travelling to far-off places. You could be Zayn's:

Official photographer

You have the creative flair needed to make sure Zayn and the boys are always seen in the best possible light. And your love of exotic places will make for some gorgeous settings.

★ SAGITTARIUS (23rd November – 21st December) ★

You're a true free spirit! You're sporty, cool and bursting with enthusiasm and new ideas. You could be Zayn's:

Tour buddy
Life on the road can be tough, but with you around, Zayn would always have a cool companion to keep him smiling.

★ CAPRICORN (22nd December – 20th January) ★
You like to take charge, and you're good at it, too. You're sensible with your cash and work harder than anyone. But you're also friendly and approachable. You could be Zayn's:

Business manager
Let's face it - pop stars aren't always the best at handling their cash! With your help, Zayn will be able to make the most of his millions. Have fun with all that dosh!

★ AQUARIUS (21st January – 19th February) ★
You're smart and logical, but also have a creative side. You love music and learning new things, and you can't stand to sit still. You could be Zayn's:

Choreographer
With your logical mind and love of music, you'd be fabulous at thinking up dynamic new dance moves for the boys.

★ PISCES (20th February – 20th March) ★
You've got a great imagination and love putting your talents to good use by making beautiful homemade gifts. You could be Zayn's:

Stage designer
You could turn the 1D boys' empty stage into a spectacular work of art. There's no way Zayn would be able to ignore your show-stopping creativity.

ZAYN TELLS HIS FANS THAT THEY ARE THE BEST IN THE
WORLD, BUT THERE'S NO DENYING THEY CAN GET A BIT
CRAZY SOMETIMES. TRY TO WORK OUT WHICH OF THESE
FAN FACTS ARE TRUE AND WHICH ARE FALSE. CHECK
YOUR ANSWERS ON **PAGE 91**.

1. Following Zayn's comment that he would love someone
to give him a superpower, one adoring fan decided to
attach a life-sized cut-out of Zayn, wearing a cape, to a
bunch of helium balloons. She let her creation fly high
into the sky, and no one has seen it since.

☐ True Tale   ☐ Fan Fake

2. A group of fans in the USA decided to hide in a bin
for four hours in the hope that they would meet
the band when the bins were brought into a venue.
Unfortunately, they were caught when it was noticed
that the bins were suspiciously heavy.

☐ True Tale   ☐ Fan Fake

3. BBC radio presenter Gemma Cairney shaved the 1D
logo into the back of her head. She also performed the
'Gangnam Style' dance with Liam Payne.

☐ True Tale   ☐ Fan Fake

4. One ultra-dedicated fan in Montreal, Canada, won't use any stationery that doesn't have Zayn's picture on it! Bad news if she forgets her favourite pens and pencils for an exam.

  ☐ True Tale   ☐ Fan Fake

5. Fans in New York, USA, queued overnight to be the first to get their hands on a copy of the second 1D album. The kind people of NYC thought that the weary fans were homeless and offered them sandwiches and blankets.

  ☐ True Tale   ☐ Fan Fake

6. A super-fan farmer from Devon, England, loved Zayn so much that he decided to put cardboard Zayn masks on his entire flock of sheep. He sent Zayn a photo of the sheepy lookalikes, but Zayn was so creeped out by it that he couldn't even look at it!

  ☐ True Tale   ☐ Fan Fake

7. A fan in New York, USA, fainted while holding Zayn's hand at a book-signing. She had to be carried off to receive medical attention – but not from Zayn, as that might have made matters worse.

  ☐ True Tale   ☐ Fan Fake

8. Zayn once started to choke on a chewy sweet during an interview in London, England. A fan leapt to his aid and helped him, saving the poorly popstar's life.

  ☐ True Tale   ☐ Fan Fake

9. A mega fan from California, USA, was so devastated when Zayn left Twitter that she refused to eat until Zayn came back. Luckily for her, Zayn decided to tweet again two days later.

☐ True Tale   ☐ Fan Fake

10. Zayn was sent a Borat-style mankini by an adoring fan. He couldn't wait to wear it, saying, 'I fully intend on wearing it when I next go swimming.' He never braved the water, but did decide to wear it around the house. He described it as 'very comfortable'.

☐ True Tale   ☐ Fan Fake

11. A fan from Brisbane, Australia, once arranged for a puppy to be sent to Zayn. The fashionable pooch was styled to imitate Zayn's look, with a blonde streak on his head, high-top trainers and a baseball jacket. The lovelorn girl attached her phone number to the puppy's collar. After naming the dog Great Zayn, the boys returned him to his owner.

☐ True Tale   ☐ Fan Fake

12. A group of fans from Mexico City, Mexico, sent Zayn a CD of Cyprus Hill's song 'Insane In The Membrane'. They had dubbed over the song with Zayn's name. That really is insane in the Zayn!

☐ True Tale   ☐ Fan Fake

FAKE!

Favourite things

THINK YOU KNOW WHAT MAKES ZAYN TICK? TRY THIS
FUN QUIZ TO SEE IF YOU KNOW ZAYN'S FAVOURITE
THINGS. THEN CHECK YOUR ANSWERS ON **PAGE 91**.

1. What is Zayn's favourite food?
   a. Cranberries
   b. Chicken
   c. Bread

2. What is Zayn's favourite country?
   a. England
   b. USA
   c. France

3. How would Zayn's favourite perfume smell?
   a. Sweet
   b. Spicy
   c. Citrussy

4. What is Zayn's ideal method of transport?
   a. Skateboard
   b. Helicopter
   c. Car

5. Zayn's a cheesy lad, but what's his favourite?
   a. Cheddar
   b. Halloumi
   c. Every type of cheese

6. Brainy Zayn was a bit of a star student at school. What was his favourite subject?
   a. French
   b. Design Technology
   c. English

7. He's a big fan of American food, but what would Zayn rather eat?
   a. Pretzels
   b. Hot dogs
   c. Apple pie

8. Obviously Zayn is a mega-celeb himself, but what other celebrity does he most admire?
   a. Adele
   b. Ed Sheeran
   c. Prince Harry

9. Everyone loves a lazy Sunday. What would be Zayn's favourite way to spend his?
   a. Watching DVDs
   b. In the sauna at the gym
   c. In bed

10. What is Zayn's favourite part of his body? It must have been difficult to pick only one!

   a. Hair

   b. Jaw line

   c. Arms

11. What is Zayn's favourite song? Suprisingly, it's not one of his own!

   a. 'Thriller' by Michael Jackson

   b. 'Let It Be' by The Beatles

   c. 'God Only Knows' by The Beach Boys

12. What is Zayn's favourite boy band of all time?

   a. The Beatles

   b. *NSYNC

   c. Take That

13. Get ready to swoon ... what's Zayn's favourite trait in a girl?

   a. Good dress sense

   b. Brown eyes

   c. Intelligence

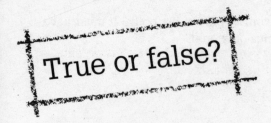

True or false?

IN THIS CUNNING QUIZ, TICK WHETHER YOU THINK
THE STATEMENTS ARE TRUE OR FALSE. BUT HERE'S
THE TWIST — YOU'LL GET AN EXTRA MARK IF YOU
CAN GUESS WHICH OTHER BAND MEMBER THE FALSE
STATEMENTS REFER TO. WRITE HIS NAME ON THE
DOTTED LINE, AND CHECK THE ANSWERS ON **PAGE 92**.

1. Zayn is a Capricorn.

☐ True   ☐ False. It is ....

2. Zayn has an older brother called Gregg.

☐ True   ☐ False. It is ....

3. Zayn's name means 'beautiful'.

☐ True   ☐ False. It is ....

4. Brainy Zayn took his English GCSE a year early and
scored an A.

☐ True   ☐ False. It is ....

5. Zayn was an early Christmas present for his parents, and was born on Christmas Eve.

☐ True   ☐ False. It is ....

6. Zayn has a double-jointed thumb.

☐ True   ☐ False. It is ....

7. Zayn was born in Wolverhampton.

☐ True   ☐ False. It was ....

8. Zayn is a sucker for a soppy romantic movie. His favourites are *Love Actually* and *Titanic*.

☐ True   ☐ False. It is ....

9. Zayn first auditioned for *The X Factor* when he was 14 years old. He reached the judges' houses stage but didn't get through.

☐ True   ☐ False. It was ....

10. Zayn's celebrity crush is Megan Fox.

☐ True   ☐ False. It is ....

What's your theme song?

You'll get all your mates together to make bunting and personalized decorations.

You want to hire an amazing venue and invite the entire school.

How will you decorate your venue?

You'll choose a funky theme to make it a party to remember.

Start
It's your birthday and it's time to party! What kind of bash do you want?

Something chilled and relaxed with only your closest friends.

Should there be dancing?

Your friends can dance if they want to, but you feel too embarrassed.

Absolutely! You can't wait to strut your stuff, even if it's just in your bedroom.

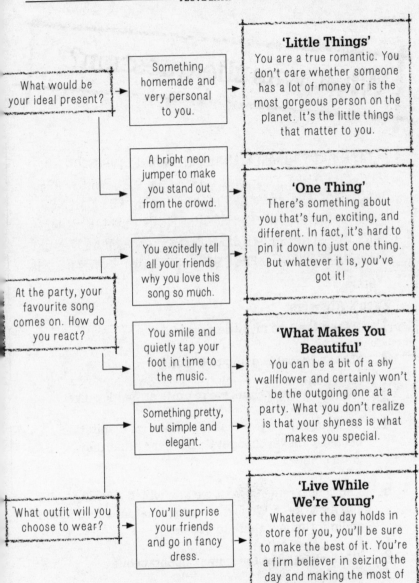

What would be your ideal present?

Something homemade and very personal to you.

'Little Things'
You are a true romantic. You don't care whether someone has a lot of money or is the most gorgeous person on the planet. It's the little things that matter to you.

A bright neon jumper to make you stand out from the crowd.

'One Thing'
There's something about you that's fun, exciting, and different. In fact, it's hard to pin it down to just one thing. But whatever it is, you've got it!

At the party, your favourite song comes on. How do you react?

You excitedly tell all your friends why you love this song so much.

You smile and quietly tap your foot in time to the music.

'What Makes You Beautiful'
You can be a bit of a shy wallflower and certainly won't be the outgoing one at a party. What you don't realize is that your shyness is what makes you special.

Something pretty, but simple and elegant.

What outfit will you choose to wear?

You'll surprise your friends and go in fancy dress.

'Live While We're Young'
Whatever the day holds in store for you, you'll be sure to make the best of it. You're a firm believer in seizing the day and making the most of every moment.

What was the question?

ZAYN HAS PROBABLY ANSWERED MORE QUESTIONS IN HIS LIFE THAN YOU COULD THINK TO ASK. BELOW ARE SOME OF THE ANSWERS HE HAS GIVEN, BUT CAN YOU MATCH EACH ONE TO ITS QUESTION? BEWARE, SOME FAKE QUESTIONS HAVE BEEN INSERTED TO MAKE IT MORE DIFFICULT! TURN TO **PAGE 92** TO FIND OUT HOW YOU DID.

Zayn's Answers:

1. 'When I talk to my little sister.'

2. 'That's probably going to be me.'

3. 'We don't really think we're quite at that level yet.'

4. 'Growing up I never looked at them for inspiration because I never thought I'd be doing what they were doing.'

5. 'Our music reflects what we are, which is young, wild and a bit crazy. We just try to get that into our music and get that out there to people.'

6. 'We just feel it at the time ... spontaneous.'

Questions:

A. Who looks in the mirror the most?

B. Do you ever hijack each other's Facebook or Twitter accounts?

C. If any of you were to go solo, who would it be?

D. Do you look up to any bands?

E. Do you have any favourite moves?

F. Do you have any particular chat-up lines you use on the ladies?

G. What do you make of the phenomenom One Direction has created?

H. Can you think of anything that would make the band split?

I. What does the future hold for One Direction?

J. What makes you smile the most?

K. What inspires you?

L. How do you feel about being compared to The Beatles?

Write your answers here:

1. ....   3. ....   5. ....

2. ....   4. ....   6. ....

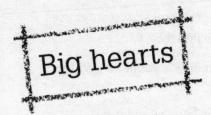

Big hearts

ZAYN'S A BIG SOFTIE AT HEART AND HAS A LOT OF LOVE FOR HIS FAMILY, FRIENDS, FANS AND CHARITABLE CAUSES. HERE ARE SOME STORIES THAT WILL MAKE YOU GO, 'AHH'. JUST FOR FUN, WHY NOT RATE THEM ON OUR 'CUTE-O-METER' SCALE?

Cute-O-Meter

Aww!

What A Cutie!

Super Sweet

Cuteness Overload

I Can't Even Cope With How Cute This Is!

Zayn loves his band mates like brothers, and has admitted to feeling protective of Niall, making sure he is safe when their fans sometimes get a little too wild. 'I don't know what it is,' says Zayn, 'but even though he isn't the youngest, he's the one we feel almost maternal towards.'

When asked what makes him smile, Zayn said, 'When I talk to my little sister.' What a great brother!

Zayn dotes on the 1D boys so much that he sends them text messages when they're apart. 'When we're not together,' he says, 'we send each other messages saying, "I really miss you." I know that sounds really girlie, but that level of closeness is important.'

He may seem too cool for school, but Zayn has admitted to being a little bit of a geek by collecting comic books when he was younger.

Band mate Harry can certainly rely on Zayn for understanding. In response to newspaper gossip about

Harry's romances, Zayn remarked, 'He is the baby of the group, but people seem to forget that because of the way that he is and that he is so charming. So it is a little bit upsetting sometimes if you see him with the weight of the world on his shoulders. It does annoy us a bit. He's a young kid and people are just giving him grief for no reason.'

Despite initially auditioning for *The X Factor* as a solo artist, Zayn has admitted that there is no way he could have dealt with fame on his own. He says, 'I would have cracked up and given it all up and gone home by now. The lads keep me grounded, and it's good to know you're not the only person going through everything. We're sharing every experience.'

If he had one day left on Earth, Zayn says he would go home and spend it with his family and friends.

It turns out that Zayn is a little superstitious. He has a necklace that he was given by someone close to him. He wears it every day and feels that it brings him good luck.

Zayn, along with the other 1D lads, is an ambassador for Rays of Sunshine – a charity that grants wishes for seriously ill children in the UK.

Zayn loves his family to pieces. When asked what makes him happiest, he said, 'When I'm home doing the most normal things. If I could go home tomorrow, I'd wake up late afternoon, come downstairs, sit on my sofa and watch TV and hang out with my family. I'd also take my sisters out shopping because I love seeing their reactions when I buy them stuff. I love seeing them happy.'

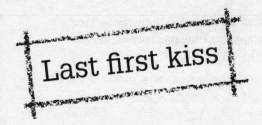

Last first kiss

ZAYN HASN'T EXACTLY GOT A FLIRTATIOUS STREAK TO RIVAL THAT OF HIS CHEEKY BAND MATE HARRY, BUT HE'S NO STRANGER TO THE WORLD OF RELATIONSHIPS. HERE ARE SOME THOUGHTS ON LOVE, ROMANCE AND WHAT HE DOES – AND DOESN'T – LOOK FOR IN A GIRL.

At a photoshoot for *Cosmopolitan* magazine in November 2012, Zayn was asked if his girlfriend helps to build his confidence. Zayn said:

'Behind every great man there's a great woman, and she's great.'

Even 1D's token Romeo, Harry, reckons Zayn is the real Prince Charming of the bunch:

'I think the most typically good-looking guy is Zayn, with the cheekbones and the jaw.'

Zayn used to think he had it all sussed out when it came to what he looked for in a girl – colour of hair and eyes and so on. Nowadays, that's not so important:

'Obviously you've got to be attracted to someone to be in a relationship, but at the same time it's [appearance] not a massive deal.'

It's safe to say Zayn definitely goes for personality over looks. In fact, it seems to be something he feels quite passionate about:

'I wouldn't say I've got a specific type when it comes to girls. I've become a lot less shallow as I've got older, and personality is very important to me now. Someone can be the best-looking person in the world, but if they're boring there's nothing worse. You have to have something to stimulate you mentally.'

So what does Zayn find attractive in a girl?

'Someone who looks after themselves and has a bit of confidence is attractive, but we've got to be friends as well.'

And let's not forget that Zayn's perfect lady would also be someone just as chilled as he is:

'Someone who's chilled out and doesn't take themselves too seriously, and who wouldn't have a hissy fit over little things. I like a girl who enjoys simple things.'

Although the world of romance interests Zayn now, he can attest that this wasn't always the case:

'I had my first kiss when I was about nine or ten years old. It was only a peck but I was paranoid that people would find out. I thought people would know just from looking at me that I'd kissed someone.'

Good news, ladies! If it doesn't work out with his current girlfriend, Zayn might be on the market for that special girl to settle down with. When asked where he'd want to be in five years' time, he said:

"I'd like One Direction to still be going and I'd like our fan base to have grown. I'd also like my own house and I'll possibly be settling down and looking to get married."

Zayn claims that his popularity began at an early age when he moved schools:

"Our new school was a lot more mixed, so I felt like I fitted in much better. Also, all the girls wanted to know who this new kid was, and that's when I became cool."

When did Zayn's love-life really begin? As ever, he's a modest lad when it comes to his popularity with the girls:

"My real interest in girls started when I was about 12 or 13. Girls would come up and ask if I wanted to go out with their friend. I had my first real girlfriend at around 15, and I was with her for about nine months. I've only ever had two or three proper girlfriends."

Sweet tweets

WE ALL KNOW ZAYN'S A REAL SWEETIE AND HE LIKES TO SHARE HIS LOVE WITH FANS, FAMILY AND FRIENDS VIA THE INTERNET.

I love the fact I grew up wanting a brother and now I have four love u boys man :)

....

Can't get over you guys. Don't get how much you amaze me. Thank you for everything, you truly are the best fans in the world. Love you all x

....

LA is definitely one of my favorite places to stay love this place :) x

....

If the love is real it will rise above all else ! :) x

....

However many amazing things happen in your life you should always be thankful for it, remain humble, modest and respectful :) x

....

That show was incredible ! And all because of you guys thanks for being so amazing :) love zayn x

....

MiSs my mummy .. X

....

Ah Yeah, A massive Happy 10th Bday to my little Sister Safaa today x

Diary dash

HAVE YOU EVER WANTED TO STAR IN YOUR OWN STORY
WITH ZAYN? WELL NOW'S YOUR CHANCE. FILL IN THE
BLANKS WITH THE WORDS SUGGESTED OR USE YOUR
OWN TO MAKE YOUR STORY SPECIAL.

You flip the page of your science book and tap your pen
against the desk. It wasn't the best idea to come to the
library on a Saturday afternoon, but you have so much
homework to do.

You'd much rather be ....
(reading poetry/ drawing/ writing a historical essay) instead.
Sighing heavily, you decide it's time for a break and wander

over to the .... (poetry/ art/
history) section.

You are running your fingers along the spines of the old,
tattered books when you come across a leather-bound
notebook sitting on top of one of the shelves. That
definitely isn't a library book. You flick through the pages.
It's some sort of organizer. Inside, you see:

Monday 11am: ....
(rehearsal/ pool party/ breakfast) *at Harry's house.*

Tuesday 1pm: .... (interview/
photoshoot/ lunch) *with Loud! magazine – call Louis.*

Wednesday 2pm: At ....
(studio/ sound-check/ hairdresser) *– take Liam's jacket.*

Thursday 1pm: Meeting with ....
(tour manager/ personal trainer/ choreographer) *– pick up Niall.*

You flick to the front of the book and gasp when you read:

.... ('Property
of Zayn Malik'/ 'Zayn's diary – hands off!'/ 'This belongs to
Zayn') on the inside cover. You've just found Zayn's diary!

You quickly turn the pages to today's date:

Saturday 2pm: .... (album-signing/
acoustic gig/ meet and greet) *at* Hot Tunes Music.

That's the music shop in town. You could go there and return

Zayn's diary to him! Feeling .... (excited/
giddy/ determined), you dash out of the library. It's a bus ride
to the music shop, and your heart is thudding all the way.

When you get off the bus and see the the music shop, your
heart sinks. The queue is halfway down the street!

Suddenly you notice your best friend, ...
(your best friend's name), is in the queue, too. She's

clutching ....

'You're here!' she cries. 'Are you excited? I can't wait to

meet .... !' (name of 1D band member)

'I wasn't expecting to come today,' you say honestly. 'But something .... (exciting/ crazy/ unbelievable) has just happened. Can you keep a secret?'

You tell her about finding Zayn's diary. She .... (looks at you in disbelief/ squeals in delight/ looks a little jealous) As you chat together, the queue moves quickly. Before you know it, you are next in line to meet the 1D boys. You can hardly contain your excitement.

When the security guard lets you through, you give the boys your most .... (dazzling smile/ cheeky wink/ cheesy grin) and make a beeline for Zayn. He gives you a friendly grin. His big brown eyes make your knees start to wobble.

'Hey,' he says. '...' (Do you want me to sign something?/ Wow! You have a great smile!/ Aren't you that famous supermodel?)

Without a word, you hand over his diary. 'My diary!' he cries. 'I thought I'd lost this. Where did you find it?'

'In the library,' you squeak. You're .... (feeling quite nervous/ absolutely terrified/ still in shock), but Zayn seems so friendly and easy to talk to.

'How can I ever thank you?' he says. 'Hang on. Let me finish up here and you can meet the other lads.'

Your heart starts to thunder wildly. 'Can I bring my best friend?' you blurt out.

'... ,' says Zayn.

In a daze, you hurry over to ....
(your best friend's name), who has been waiting for you. You excitedly tell her Zayn's amazing offer. She is thrilled.

It's not long before the 1D boys finish with their fans, and you follow them upstairs to a large room with comfy

.... (sofas/ beanbags/ hammocks)
and tables of drinks and sweets.

Then suddenly, Zayn is standing next to you, with the rest of the boys gathered behind him. 'Guys,' he says, 'this is

.... (your name). She's the one I was telling you about.'

The rest of the band greet you like an old friend. Liam and Louis .... (hug you/ shake your hand), Niall .... (gives you a high five/ squeezes your shoulder) and Harry ....
.... (kisses you on the hand/ gives you a bear hug)

'I don't know quite how to thank you,' says Zayn. 'But I wondered if you and your friend would like free backstage passes to our next show?'

'Yes!' you both cry together. What ....
(an amazing/ a weird/ a crazy) day. Who'd have thought that only this afternoon you were doing your homework and now you're hanging out with One Direction!

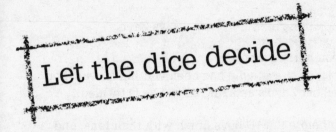

Let the dice decide

GET READY TO DISCOVER YOUR DESTINY WITH ZAYN.
THIS IS A FUN GAME THAT YOU CAN PLAY AGAIN AND
AGAIN — ALL YOU NEED IS A DICE. GET ROLLING AND
FOLLOW THE INSTRUCTIONS BELOW TO SEE INTO
THE FUTURE.

1. Create your own suggestions for where you'll meet
and what you'll do together, and write them in the
'Your choice' section for categories **A** to **E**.

2. Roll the dice once for each of the categories. The
number you roll is the option the dice has chosen
for you.

3. Write down your future with Zayn in the box on the
opposite page and wait to see if it comes true.

CATEGORIES

A. Where you and Zayn will meet:
1. At the aquarium **2.** At an art gallery **3.** In the library
4. At a music festival **5.** At a vintage market

6. (Your choice) ....

B. What you will do together:
1. Have a candlelit dinner **2.** Go for a picnic in the park
3. Go on a tour of London **4.** Take a trip to a chocolate
factory **5.** Go shoe shopping

6. (Your choice) ....

C. He will think you're so:
1. Intelligent **2.** Funny **3.** Mysterious **4.** Talented **5.** Sweet

6. (Your choice) ....

D. What he will give you as a gift:
1. A song he's written for you **2.** A lock of his wonderfully
styled hair **3.** A dozen red roses **4.** An expensive perfume
5. A backstage pass to his show

6. (Your choice) ....

E. Where you and Zayn will go:
1. Los Angeles **2.** New Zealand **3.** Paris **4.** Disneyland
5. Japan

6. (Your choice) ....

Your future with Zayn:

I'm going to meet Zayn ....

Together, we will ....

He will think I am ....

As a gift, he will give me ....

We'll travel to ....

Guess who?

READ THE QUOTES FROM ZAYN BELOW AND SEE IF YOU CAN WORK OUT WHO OR WHAT HE IS TALKING ABOUT. SEE IF YOU'VE CRACKED THE CLUES BY CHECKING YOUR ANSWERS ON PAGE 92.

1. 'I bonded with him really quickly because he's like me in a lot of ways.'

Clue: A One Direction band mate that shares his name with an *X Factor* judge.

Who is it? ....

2. 'She still cries every time I go home and leave again.'

Clue: Ever the family man, Zayn will always have this special lady in his life.

Who is it? ....

3. 'He is a cheeky chappy.'

Clue: This curly-haired chap has a lot of style.

Who is it? ....

4. 'I wasn't into that kind of music, but I was totally converted as soon as I met him. He's got an aura about him and it's very evident when he walks into a room.'

Clue: Would you let this music legend entertain you?

Who is it? ....

5. 'He's so much fun and he never stops. It must be exhausting being him.'

Clue: A cheeky Irish charmer and a true best mate.

Who is it? ....

6. 'Such a funny dude!'

Clue: Outrageous comedian and star of *The Dictator*.

Who is it? ....

7. 'He's quite serious and focused.'

Clue: Although he's not the oldest, this band member acts like the big brother of the group, and often keeps the rest of the boys in check.

Who is it? ....

8. 'You truly were a legend.'

Clue: This thrilling music idol certainly wasn't bad in Zayn's eyes.

Who is it? ....

9. 'I used to do it in front of my sisters when they were younger to freak them out.'

Clue: Zayn's handy (and gross!) party trick.

What is it? ....

10. 'I had a bit of a thing for them and for a while I always used to buy things when we went through airports. They cost a fortune!'

Clue: No kidding! Not many people can afford this great, gorgeous, gifted, glorious designer with a G-shaped logo.

Who is it? ....

11. 'There's a Nintendo DS and we've got a console on there so we keep ourselves entertained.'

Clue: A super-stylish mode of transport for when the boys are on tour.

What is it? ....

12. 'I'd never even seen one before I joined One Direction, so to be touring around and seeing lots of different countries, it's amazing.'

Clue: Now Zayn's finally got a passport, he's sure to be flying high with happiness.

What is it? ....

Twitterverse

ZAYN MAY BE ON TOP OF THE WORLD OF POP, BUT IT'S EASY
TO SEE FROM HIS TWEETS THAT HE'S JUST LIKE ANY OTHER
GUY — SWEET, COOL AND SOMETIMES A LITTLE BIT WACKY.

I either wanna cut my hair short or grow it really long what dya think ? X

Ordering pizza an it's sounding good ;) x

Playing a bit of guitar before bed. Up early tomorrow. What are you guys up to tonight :) x

Yawn :/ sleeptime now for real x

Shoo bop shoobidee bop de shoo bop ! :) x

this bath is amazing :) thumbs up aha

really happy today :D Avocado is my new fave vegetable :) x

wow our fans are vats zapennin ! you guys are amazing ! :) x

Weathers been wicked today. Nothing like having your tea outside on a cool night x

Cringe!

ZAYN MIGHT SEEM TO BE THE COOLEST GUY ON EARTH, BUT EVEN HE CAN HAVE EMBARRASSING MOMENTS. READ THESE STORIES OF SHAME, AND DECIDE WHETHER EACH ONE IS A TRUE CRINGE, OR A FAKE FAIL. YOU CAN CHECK YOUR ANSWERS ON **PAGE 92**.

1. When Zayn was six years old he cut all his hair off with a pair of scissors. When his teacher put the hair into an envelope and told him he had to go home and tell his mother, he used PVA glue to stick it back on again.

☐ True Cringe   ☐ Fake Fail

2. Zayn started driving lessons when he was 17 years old, but he has failed his driving test five times ... so far!

☐ True Cringe   ☐ Fake Fail

3. Zayn had never been out of the country and didn't even own a passport until he got through to the judges' houses stage of *The X Factor* and went to Marbella.

☐ True Cringe   ☐ Fake Fail

4. Zayn had to stand on a brick for his first kiss. The lucky girl was so much taller than him that he couldn't reach her lips without it!

☐ True Cringe   ☐ Fake Fail

5. When Zayn was seven years old, he told his friends at school that he had caught the tooth fairy underneath a flowerpot. When he revealed what he had caught, it turned out to be a small bat!

☐ True Cringe   ☐ Fake Fail

6. When Zayn was younger, he thought it was very cool to shave slits into his eyebrows and wear baggy jogging bottoms and hoodies all the time to try and look 'gangsta'.

☐ True Cringe   ☐ Fake Fail

7. Once, when flying to Los Angeles, Zayn was taken to the back room of the airport and interviewed for an hour because his name was similar to that of someone passport control was looking for.

☐ True Cringe   ☐ Fake Fail

8. Zayn was very creative as a child. He loved painting so much that while his dog was asleep, he painted her fur bright yellow.

☐ True Cringe   ☐ Fake Fail

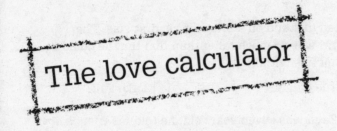

The love calculator

HERE'S A FAST AND FUN WAY TO WORK OUT WHETHER YOU ARE ZAYN'S PERFECT MATCH.

Write down your name and Zayn's with the word 'LOVES' in the middle. Then write down how many times the letters L, O, V, E and S appear in both your names in a line – but don't include the letters from 'LOVES'. Add together each pair of numbers – the first and the second, the second and the third, and so on – to work out a final 'percentage'. This tells you how likely you are to be Zayn's dream girl.

Here's an example:

BRYONY JONES LOVES ZAYN MALIK

There are one L, two Os, zero Vs, one E and one S.

Write this as: 1 2 0 1 1

Add together each pair of numbers until you only have two left:

1 2 0 1 1
3 2 1 2
5 3 3
86%

Spot the difference

Can you find eight differences between the top and bottom pictures? You can check your answers on page 93.

Clowning around

ARE YOU READY TO TAKE CENTRE STAGE IN A ZAYN
MALIK ADVENTURE? READ THE STORY BELOW AND
CHOOSE YOUR OPTIONS CAREFULLY.
WHAT WILL HAPPEN NEXT? YOU DECIDE!

As a juggler in a professional circus, sometimes you feel
like the luckiest person in the world. But that doesn't stop
your parents from making sure you keep up with your
school work, or clean up after the elephants.

The circus doesn't have a show for two weeks, and
you've already practised your routine to death. You sit
around, feeling glum, watching your parents practise their
trapeze act.

'Don't look so fed up!' Mum calls, adjusting her sparkling
costume. 'Your dad has some great news to tell you.'

'What's the news, Dad?' you ask.

'We have a special show to prepare for tonight,' he says.
'A very famous band were meant to be playing at a venue
in town, but it's flooded, so the band are coming here
instead.'

'Wow!' you say. 'Which band?'

'I don't know,' he says. 'But I just spoke to their manager on the phone. She says that they've decided to give tonight's gig a circus theme, to fit in with its new venue. That's where you come in. One of the band needs to learn to juggle as soon as possible.'

'What's his name?' you ask.

'Zayn Malik,' he says.

OMG, it's One Direction!

If you decide:

1. To faint clean away, go to **A**, below.

2. To grab your juggling balls and tell your dad you're the best person for the job, go to **B**, on **page 55**.

A: You sit up in a daze. You must have fainted! Your mum and dad are standing over you with worried looks on their faces. They don't look happy.

'I can do it,' you tell them. 'It's One Direction!'

Your mum shakes her head. 'It's too much excitement for you,' she says. 'You should go to bed right now and rest.'

'But who will teach Zayn to juggle?' you ask.

'One of the clowns can do it,' she says. 'We can't have you fainting all over the place. No arguments.'

Oh no, you can't believe you fainted and ruined your chance of meeting Zayn and the rest of 1D.

If you decide:

1. To nod your head sadly and go to your bed, go to **A1**, below.

2. To argue with your mum and dad about their decision, go to **A2**, on **page 52**.

A1: You nod your head sadly and go to your family's trailer. Once you're inside, you curl up on your bed and start to cry.

You'd give anything to meet Zayn. He's your favourite member of One Direction. And even though the very thought of him makes you feel faint, all over again, you can't believe your parents could be so mean!

As you get more and more annoyed, you decide you must come up with a plan. It's just not fair that you should stay in bed while everyone else at the circus is enjoying seeing One Direction perform live. What will your friends say when they find out the boys came to your circus and you didn't even get to meet them?

But what should your plan be?

What do you do?

1. If you decide to disguise yourself as a clown to teach Zayn to juggle, go to **A1a**, on **page 52**.

2. If you decide to sneak out and steer well clear of your parents, go to **A1b**, on **page 53**.

A2: 'No,' you tell your dad. 'I'm teaching Zayn to juggle and you can't stop me!'

Your dad frowns. 'Don't be so rude,' he says.

'But you won't let me meet Zayn!' you yell. 'He's my idol.'

'That's it,' your dad fumes. 'You're grounded. You can't come to the show at all!'

You stomp off to your family's trailer in a huff. Your dad is so unfair. You can't believe he won't let you teach Zayn to juggle or see One Direction perform.

In the trailer you almost start to cry, but then you look out of the window and see something ...

What do you see?

1. If you see Zayn outside, go to **A2a**, on **page 54**.

2. If you see five clowns, go to **A2b**, on **page 54**.

A1a: You head out of your trailer and go to the dressing room. It's an amazing place filled with colourful wigs, bright costumes and loads of make up.

You make up your face with white paint and a bright red smile, and pull on a costume and a bright yellow wig. Your parents will never recognize you dressed like this!

As you walk back to the tent, someone grabs you by the elbow, taking you by surprise. 'Excuse me,' they say. 'Are you the one that's going to teach me how to juggle?'

You turn your bright yellow, curly head. It's Zayn! 'Yes!' you squeak. 'Follow me.'

You lead Zayn into the tent and spend the whole afternoon teaching him how to juggle. You're laughing so much that you don't even notice when your dad walks in.

He pulls off your wig. 'Did you really think I wouldn't recognize you?' he says, laughing. At least he's not angry.

'She's saved my skin for this show,' says Zayn. 'She's a great juggler and I've never seen a prettier clown!'

THE END

A1b: You sneak back into the tent and there you see Bob the clown with none other than Zayn Malik, teaching him to juggle. But he's not as good as you!

'Bob,' you say, striding over. 'I'll take it from here.'

Zayn gives you a dazzling smile. 'You're that amazing juggler I've heard so much about,' he says.

But one look into Zayn's lovely brown eyes, and you feel your legs turning to jelly. You faint again!

When you come around, both Zayn, Bob and your dad are kneeling over you. You're so embarrassed!

'Well, I guess I can't keep you away from Zayn,' your dad laughs. He can see you're so mortified that he lets you stay with Zayn and teach him your amazing juggling moves.

THE END

A2a: You dash to the window and open it. 'Hey!' you shout.

Zayn looks in your direction. He jogs over to the window. He's wearing a black and white sports jacket and bright red high-top trainers. He looks so cool!

'What's going on?' he says.

'This is going to sound really weird,' you say. 'I'm meant to be teaching you how to juggle today, but my dad's grounded me.'

'Is there any reason you can't teach me to juggle in the trailer?' he says. To your amazement, he walks over to the door and comes in.

He gives you a dazzling smile and pulls five new juggling balls out of his pocket. 'I've heard you're one of the best jugglers in the country,' he says. 'So I got the rest of the 1D lads to sign these for you, to say thank you.'

Wow! You can't believe it. Not only do you get to spend the entire day teaching Zayn to juggle after all, you also have an amazing souvenir to remind you of this day, forever.

THE END

A2b: You dash out of the trailer and stride over to the unfamiliar clowns. 'Hey,' you call, 'who are you?'

The clowns all turn to face you with big grins on their faces. One of them pulls off his wig, and there's no mistaking that magnificent quiff – it's Zayn Malik, and the rest of the clowns are the other ID boys!

'Hi,' he says. 'We're performing a show tonight and thought we'd get into the circus spirit. Are you the one who's going to teach me how to juggle?'

'Yes,' you say, dazzled by Zayn's good looks, even dressed as a clown. 'But my dad has grounded me.'

'Don't worry. Let us have a word with him,' says Zayn.

The 1D boys head for the tent and come back five minutes later. 'Ready to teach me some juggling?' says Zayn.

'What did you do to convince him?' you ask.

'Who could resist us, looking like this?' he smiles, and you know you're going to have an amazing day.

THE END

B: 'Great!' says your dad. He'll be here in ten minutes, so get ready.'

You wait nervously for Zayn to arrive and practise your moves. You're so nervous you keep dropping the balls! As you're picking them off the floor, you notice how tatty and old they're looking. You need something more special to impress Zayn!

You head to the supplies trailer outside and search until you find exactly what you're looking for.

What are you looking for?

1. If you're looking for fire clubs, go to **B1**, on **page 56**.

2. If you're looking for rollerskates, go to **B2**, on **page 56**.

B1: Excellent, you've found the fire clubs. You've juggled with fire lots of times before. It looks scary, but you've been through the proper training and you know exactly what you're doing.

When you go back into the tent, you find Zayn waiting for you. You give a little gasp of shock.

'Hi,' he says. 'Wow! Are you going to juggle with fire?'

'Yes,' you squeak. You'd better get this right!

You light the clubs and begin your routine. Zayn is laughing and clapping. You must look really impressive.

But then ...

What happens?

1. Disaster strikes! You set Zayn's quiff alight! Go to **B1a**, on **page 57**.

2. Your dad catches you. Go to **B1b**, on **page 58**.

B2: Great, you've found the rollerskates. You've never roller skated and juggled at the same time before, but how difficult can it be?

Once you're out of the trailer, you strap on the skates and zoom towards the tent. You're going pretty fast and seem to be speeding up. Uh oh – you realize you're going faster and faster, and you don't know how to stop!

You hurtle into the tent, and, to your horror, you see Zayn.

He turns towards you with a look of shock on his face, but it's too late now!

'Look out!' you cry, rolling straight towards him. You squeeze your eyes shut and hope for the best ...

What happens?

1. If Zayn catches you in his arms, go to **B2a**, on **page 58**.

2. If you crash into Zayn and knock him to the floor, go to **B2b**, on **page 59**.

B1a: 'Oh no!' you scream. But luckily you act fast and grab one of the clowns' buckets of water that's sitting nearby.

You empty the entire bucket over Zayn's head. It puts out the burning quiff, but you've soaked him to the bone. You bet he's really angry.

Zayn looks down at his dripping, wet clothes and, to your relief, begins to laugh. 'I think you just saved my life,' he says.

You smile at him. 'I think I've ruined your hair,' you say.

Zayn laughs. 'That's okay. I was looking for a new look any way,' he says.

You can't believe that Zayn is such a cool guy, who doesn't even mind that you set his hair on fire! While Zayn dries off, you spend the rest of the afternoon laughing and teaching him to juggle – this time with the usual balls!

THE END

B1b: 'Hey!' your dad cries, hurrying over. 'You know you're not meant to use the fire clubs without asking!'

You feel your face flush bright red and dunk the fire clubs into a nearby bucket of water to extinguish them. 'Sorry, Dad,' you say.

'Actually,' says Zayn. 'That was the most impressive thing I've ever seen. Why don't you join us on stage tonight and show everyone what you can do?'

You gasp with delight. On stage with One Direction? You can't imagine anything better. But your dad doesn't look very happy with you.

'Can I do it, Dad?' you beg. 'Please.'

'Okay,' your dad says. 'But you still shouldn't have taken them without asking. You're lucky that Zayn can see how talented you are.'

This might be the best day ever! You spend it working on a special routine with Zayn, and that evening you storm the stage with your amazing moves. The crowd goes wild when you and Zayn perform your routine, and to top it all off, Zayn says it's the best One Direction show yet!

THE END

B2a: Zayn quickly opens his arms and catches you before you fall. You grab his shoulders and steady yourself.

Zayn laughs brightly. 'Are you okay?' he asks.

'I think so,' you mumble, your face going bright red. You're so embarrassed.

'Aren't you the one who's meant to be teaching me how to juggle?' he asks. 'What's with the rollerskates?'

'Well ... I was trying to impress you,' you say, shyly.

Zayn laughs again. 'You've certainly made an impression!' he says.

You're so relieved that Zayn is such a nice guy. You have an amazing day teaching him how to juggle, but you leave the rollerskates for another time.

THE END

B2b: SMACK! You slam right into Zayn, throwing you both into a heap on the floor. Oh no! What if he's hurt?

Zayn coughs and shakes his head. 'Are you okay?' he asks.

'I'm fine, but are you?' you ask. 'You have a show tonight.'

Zayn laughs. 'Don't worry about it,' he says, getting up and dusting himself off. 'It's not every day I get run down by such a pretty rollerskater.'

You blush and offer to start the juggling lesson.

'That would be great,' says Zayn. 'But I think you should take those skates off first!'

You spend an amazing day together, teaching Zayn how to juggle. He's a natural and impresses everyone at the show that night. And at the end of the concert, before he heads off stage, he tells the audience that he could not have done any of it without you. And then he blows you a kiss for everyone to see.

THE END

Dream date

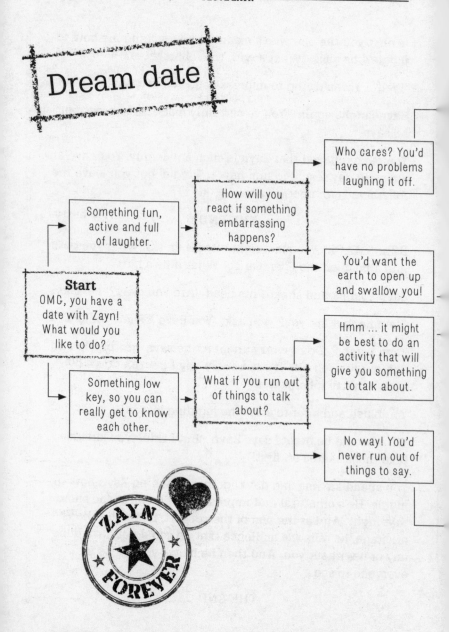

Something fun, active and full of laughter.

How will you react if something embarrassing happens?

Who cares? You'd have no problems laughing it off.

You'd want the earth to open up and swallow you!

Start
OMG, you have a date with Zayn! What would you like to do?

Something low key, so you can really get to know each other.

What if you run out of things to talk about?

Hmm ... it might be best to do an activity that will give you something to talk about.

No way! You'd never run out of things to say.

ZAYN FOREVER

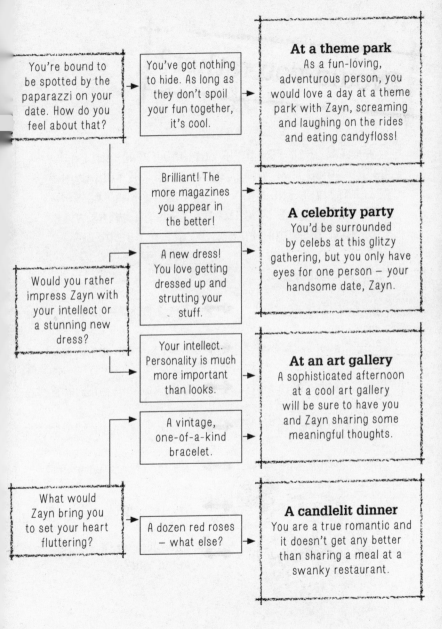

You're bound to be spotted by the paparazzi on your date. How do you feel about that?

You've got nothing to hide. As long as they don't spoil your fun together, it's cool.

At a theme park
As a fun-loving, adventurous person, you would love a day at a theme park with Zayn, screaming and laughing on the rides and eating candyfloss!

Brilliant! The more magazines you appear in the better!

A celebrity party
You'd be surrounded by celebs at this glitzy gathering, but you only have eyes for one person – your handsome date, Zayn.

Would you rather impress Zayn with your intellect or a stunning new dress?

A new dress! You love getting dressed up and strutting your stuff.

Your intellect. Personality is much more important than looks.

At an art gallery
A sophisticated afternoon at a cool art gallery will be sure to have you and Zayn sharing some meaningful thoughts.

A vintage, one-of-a-kind bracelet.

What would Zayn bring you to set your heart fluttering?

A dozen red roses – what else?

A candlelit dinner
You are a true romantic and it doesn't get any better than sharing a meal at a swanky restaurant.

Would you rather?

WHAT WOULD YOU DO IF YOU HAD THE CHANCE TO
SPEND SOME TIME WITH ZAYN? READ THE FOLLOWING
ALTERNATIVES AND MARK YOUR CHOICE FOR EACH ONE.
YOU MIGHT LIKE TO COMPARE YOUR ANSWERS WITH
THOSE OF YOUR FRIENDS TO SEE IF YOU DIFFER.

Would you rather ...

Get his autograph? ⟷ Get a lock of his hair?

Sing a duet with Zayn? ⟷ Have him serenade you?

Play Scrabble with him? ⟷ Sing karaoke with him?

Be his personal trainer? ⟷ Be his bodyguard?

Go to dinner with him? ⟷ Go for brunch with him?

Perm his hair? ⟷ Wax his legs?

Go on tour with him? ⟷ Have him write a song about you?

Be his assistant? ⟷ Be his vocal coach?

Direct a movie about him? ⟷ Be the drummer in his backing band?

Play Twister with him? ⟷ Go iceskating with him?

Paint his nails ⟷ Do his make-up?

Live next door to him? ⟷ Go to school with him?

Take a ride together in a gondola in Venice? ⟷ Go skydiving together?

Be his best friend? ⟷ Have a song he wrote about you go to the top of the charts?

See him every day for a couple of minutes? ⟷ See him once a year for a whole day?

Have him give you a wake-up call every morning? ⟷ Have him sing a lullaby to send you to sleep?

Have him give you piggybacks wherever you go? ⟷ Have him carry your bags for you for the rest of your life?

Your perfect day

IF YOU COULD GET PAID FOR DAYDREAMING ABOUT
HANGING OUT WITH ZAYN, YOU'D BE A MILLIONAIRE.
DESCRIBE YOUR PERFECT DAY WITH HIM. WHERE WOULD
YOU GO? WHAT WOULD YOU WEAR? WRITE IT ALL HERE.
THERE'S SPACE TO CONTINUE YOUR DAYDREAM ON THE
NEXT PAGES.

Need help getting started?
Try to include the answers to these questions:

- How would your day start?
- How long have you been a fan?
- What do you love most about Zayn?
- What are your favourite songs?
- Where would you take him?
- What would he wear?
- What would you eat together?
- What would you say to him?
- What would you want to ask him?
- What would you want him to ask you?
- How would your day end?

All directions!

UP, DOWN, FORWARDS, BACKWARDS, EVEN DIAGONALLY — YOU NEED TO SEARCH EVERY WHICH WAY IN THIS PUZZLE TO FIND PEOPLE, PLACES AND SONGS THAT MEAN A LOT TO ZAYN. HOW QUICKLY CAN YOU FIND THE TEN WORDS BELOW? TURN TO **PAGE 93** IF YOU GET STUCK!

ZAYN MALIK

VAS HAPPENIN'

ONE DIRECTION

BRADFORD

'LITTLE THINGS'

HARRY STYLES

LIAM PAYNE

LOUIS TOMLINSON

NIALL HORAN

THE X FACTOR

V	T	O	N	E	D	I	R	E	C	T	I	O	N	N
A	A	E	F	I	C	R	M	H	C	O	A	E	I	O
S	V	I	G	S	H	L	I	R	K	W	S	Y	A	S
H	H	C	M	E	E	I	M	H	O	S	C	V	L	N
A	A	D	O	L	T	A	I	K	B	H	E	G	L	I
P	O	Z	A	Y	N	M	A	L	I	K	M	K	H	L
P	T	F	I	T	W	P	M	I	O	U	A	C	O	M
E	T	G	K	S	F	A	D	T	M	H	G	G	R	O
N	A	E	S	Y	G	Y	G	R	A	T	R	E	A	T
I	T	E	E	R	A	N	C	S	O	K	I	L	N	S
N	A	L	L	R	F	E	D	B	C	F	C	T	H	I
M	M	D	T	A	G	T	E	D	E	N	D	A	O	U
W	F	I	I	H	D	B	N	D	H	I	L	A	M	O
T	H	E	X	F	A	C	T	O	R	F	M	B	R	L
V	S	G	N	I	H	T	E	L	T	T	I	L	N	B

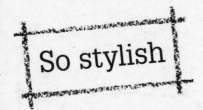

So stylish

ZAYN IS OFTEN THOUGHT TO BE THE MOST
FASHION CONSCIOUS OF THE 1D BOYS. WHEN ASKED THE
FIVE THINGS HE LAST SPENT MONEY ON, HE REPLIED,
'CLOTHES, CLOTHES, CLOTHES, CLOTHES AND CLOTHES!'

Colour in the stars to rate these Zayn looks and then pick
your ultimate favourite.

Style-O-Meter

★☆☆☆☆ Just Chilling

★★☆☆☆ Hot To Trot

★★★☆☆ Too Cool For School

★★★★☆ Style Overload

★★★★★ This Man Should Be On
The Catwalk!

Sharp and sleek

At the GQ UK Fashion Awards in 2012, Zayn really dressed up for the occasion in a tailored black suit and a pair of shoes so shiny he could probably see his reflection in them. He complemented the look with a bright white pocket square, skinny tie and striped shirt.

Standing out from the crowd

Suited and booted at the 2012 Brit Awards, Zayn showed that he isn't afraid to look different from the other lads by wearing a cream double-breasted jacket, checked shirt and shiny brogues.

Just chillin'

When Zayn wants to relax, you will either see him wrapping up warm in a cosy onesie, rocking some tracksuit bottoms, trainers and a hoodie, or — if he has to leave the house — looking slightly less casual in a polo shirt, sports jacket and jeans combo. He still manages to look effortlessly stylish by wearing clothes that fit well and accessories that he can customize. Blinging studs and necklaces add the finishing touches.

Body art

Zayn is a huge fan of tattoos. He just keeps adding more and more to his collection, getting new artworks that are symbolic and extremely personal to him.

What do you think of Zayn's tats? Rate the following tattoos out of ten, then score the tattooed look in general.

Microphone .... Crossed fingers ....

'ZAP' .... Silver fern ....

The quiff

There's no doubt about it, Zayn's hair is as impressive as hair comes, and often a talking point for Directioners looking to discuss the style of the 1D boys. An added blond streak went down very well with fans across the world when it was unleashed at the London 2012 Olympics opening ceremony. When asked about his hair, Zayn said, 'My hair takes about 25 minutes to do. It has to be blow-dried a cerain way for my quiff — I don't just wake up with it looking like this in the morning.'

High tops are top

If he was asked to name the love of his life, it wouldn't be surprising if Zayn said it was a pair of high-top trainers.

The style stud has admitted to owning a huge collection of these cool, colourful shoes, and he manages to make them work with any oufit, whether it's a formal suit or casual chinos. They certainly help with that confident swagger.

Trademark

Zayn could wear a plastic bag and still look good, but whatever look he's rocking, he's always sure to come back to his classic signature style — a baseball-type jacket (often monogrammed with 'Malik') or a cosy fitted jumper, loose trousers and, of course, his beloved high-top trainers.

Check him out

Not many people can do it, but Zayn is cool enough to pull off the trendy geek-chic style. Teaming a checked shirt with thick-rimmed black glasses, he effortlessly slips into a cool preppy style. If he wants to dress it up, he often adds a blazer or a well-cut suit with industrial boots.

Star style

Go barefoot! You can't get any more comfy than that.

Something casual, but with accessories to add some glamour.

You've been dancing for an hour and your feet are killing you. What do you do?

Find some other shoes to sling on.

Start
You're mad for Mr Malik's style, but what's your ideal party piece?

A tailored outfit that will stop the other partygoers in their tracks.

Uh oh – wardrobe malfunction! What do you do?

Salvage your outfit with whatever creative solution you can come up with.

Go home and change immediately!

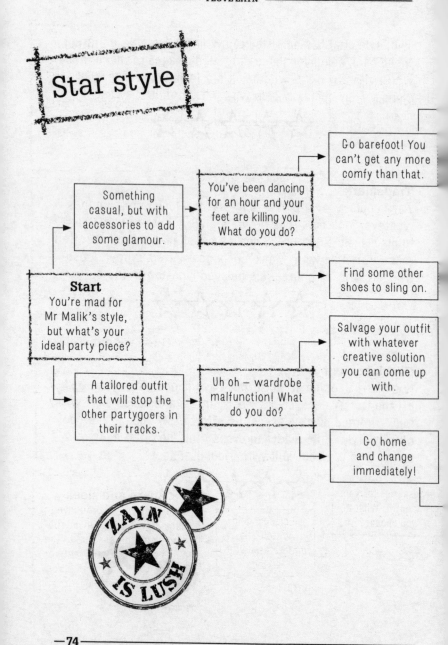

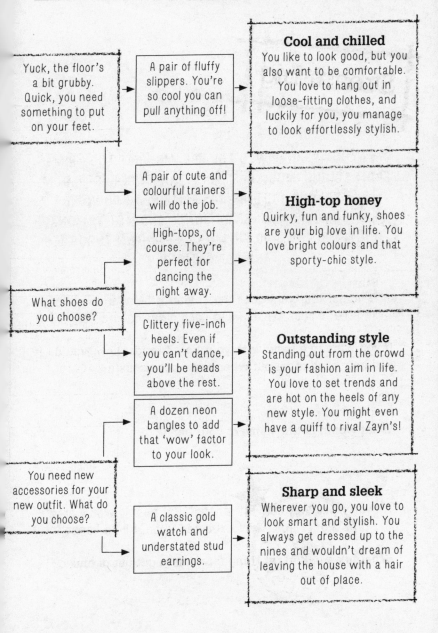

Dream big

ZAYN HAS FOLLOWED THE DREAMS THAT TOOK HIM
FROM SCHOOL MUSICALS TO INTERNATIONAL STARDOM,
BUT THROUGHOUT, HE HAS REMAINED GROUNDED.
READ SOME OF HIS INSPIRATIONAL AND MOTIVATIONAL
QUOTES BELOW AND THEN ADD YOUR OWN THOUGHTS
AND ASPIRATIONS.

'I've got four very good mates out of being in the band
and that's cool. We all keep each other down to earth.'

**If you were in a band with your best friends, how would
you help each other out when fame got stressful?**

....

What would be the name of your band?

....

'Even if we only convert a handful of people who weren't
fans before and never expected to be, I'll be happy.'

What is an important thing for a fan to get out of music?

....

Do you think it's important to try new things in life?

....

'I'm massively proud. It's just crazy to think, "Why would all these people come and see me?" It's really cool.'

Zayn loves his fans. Name a few of your biggest heroes.

....

What do you think someone has to do to earn a fan base?

....

'To be touring around and seeing lots of different countries, it's amazing.'

Where would you most like to visit in the world?

....

What other career would mean you get to travel the world?

....

'Being on stage with Robbie Williams during The X Factor was sick. He was amazing and hung out with us all day.'

What celebrity would you most like to hang out with?

....

If you were famous, what would you do with your fans?

....

'There would be no One Direction without the fans and we're so grateful that you've been there every step of the way.'

Do you think keeping fans happy is the most important thing a celebrity can do?

....

What's the most extreme thing you have done as a fan?

....

'I absolutely loved being on stage and becoming somebody else. I found being a character really liberating and I used to get such an adrenaline rush from acting.'

Before he turned his attention to singing, Zayn used to love taking to the stage to act. Do you like to be on stage?

....

What gives you a real adrenaline rush?

....

'Everything is going so fast and you're suddenly standing on red carpets and meeting famous people and singing to millions.'

What would be the best thing about being famous?

....

Do you think there are any downsides to fame?

....

'The show gave me a lot more confidence and taught me how to speak to people, and I'm really grateful for that.'

Do you ever wish you had more confidence?

....

What do you think you could do to build your confidence?

....

'I appreciate getting to spend time with my family so much more now, because when I do go home it's so fleeting that I make the most of every minute.'

Is there anything you think you take for granted?

....

If your life was to change in a whirlwind of fame, what is the one thing you'd like to remain the same?

....

Timeline

ZAYN HAS HAD AN UNBELIEVABLE RISE TO STARDOM AND
HIS FANS HAVE BEEN WITH HIM EVERY STEP OF THE WAY.
TAKE A LOOK AT THESE MAJOR MOMENTS IN HIS LIFE.

THERE ARE SOME BLANK SPACES FOR YOU TO FILL IN.
THE MISSING WORDS AND DATES ARE AT THE BOTTOM OF
PAGE 83. INSERT THEM WHERE YOU THINK THEY SHOULD
BE AND THEN CHECK YOUR ANSWERS ON **PAGE 94**.

....(1): Zayn Malik was born in
Bradford, England.

1996: Zayn's earliest memory is of going to the fair with
his grandma and mum. 'Everything seemed so big, and I
remember the bright lights and the thrill of going on the
merry-go-round.'

2005–2006: Zayn starts taking pride in his appearance and
getting up for school 30 minutes before his sisters so that
he can style his ....(2)!

June 2010: Zayn has his first audition for *The X Factor*
singing Mario's ....(3).

September 2010: After Simon Cowell forms One Direction
from individual solo singers, they perform at his house in

Marbella, singing Natalie Imbruglia's 'Torn'.

October 2010: In the first of the live shows, One Direction sings Coldplay's 'Viva la Vida' to much acclaim.

December 2010: One Direction performs with Robbie Williams during *The X Factor* live final. Zayn describes singing with Robbie as 'sick' (in a good way). They come third in the competition, losing out to winner Matt Cardle and runner-up Rebecca Ferguson. 'We're definitely going to stay together. This isn't the last of One Direction,' says Zayn.

March 2011: Zayn strikes a pose with the rest of the band as they release their first book *One Direction:*

...............................(4), which tops the bestseller list.

May 2011: Zayn and Rebecca Ferguson go public and announce that they are dating each other.

July 2011: Zayn and Rebecca split.

August 2011: Zayn arrives at the Radio 1 London studios with his band mates for the first play of One Direction's

debut single ....(5).

September 2011: Their debut single reaches No. 1 in the

UK Top 40. It goes on to spend ....(6) consecutive weeks in the charts.

February 2012: Zayn flies to the US with One Direction to begin a Stateside tour.

February 2012: One Direction wins the award for

....(7) at the Brit Awards.

The boys beat nine other acts to scoop the prize for their debut track 'What Makes You Beautiful'.

March 2012: One Direction becomes the first British group to go straight to No. 1 on the US Billboard 200 chart with their album *Up All Night*.

.................................(8): One Direction arrives in Sydney for a mini-tour of Australia and New Zealand.

May 2012: 'What Makes You Beautiful' goes double platinum in the US. The boys celebrate being one of the most successful British boy bands to make it in America.

May 2012: Zayn Malik and Little Mix's ....
(9) reveal that they are an item.

August 2012: Zayn and the One Direction boys perform 'What Makes You Beautiful' on a moving carnival float at the ....(10) in London.

August 2012: Zayn quits ....(11) – only to come back two days later.

August 2012: Zayn unveils a new blonde streak in his hair. Directioners everywhere go wild.

August 2012: 'Live While We're Young' becomes the ....(12) selling pre-order song in history.

September 2012: One Direction win three MTV Video Music Awards in Los Angeles. They beat the likes of

....(13) and Rihanna in the Best Pop

Video category for 'What Makes You Beautiful' and also collect the award for Best New Artist. Zayn says, 'We'd just like to say a massive thank you to each and every single one of you in here tonight and also to all of our fans, friends, family. And to all the people who work with us each day.' After belting out 'One Thing', they pick up their third award for Most Share-worthy Video.

November 2012: One Direction release their second album, called ....(14).

November 2012: One Direction do a UK chart double with their new single 'Little Things', reaching ....(15) and their album *Take Me Home*, doing the same.

February 2013: One Direction embark on a world tour.

August 2013: A 3D film about the boys is released across the globe, directed by none other than ....
......................(16)!

Missing words

April 2012	Olympics Closing Ceremony
Hair	*Take Me Home*
Justin Bieber	No. 1
12th January 1993	'What Makes You Beautiful'
'Forever Young'	Morgan Spurlock
19	Twitter
Perrie Edwards	'Let Me Love You'
Best British Single	Fastest

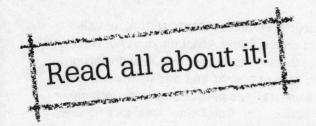

Read all about it!

THE MEDIA CAN'T GET ENOUGH OF NEWS ABOUT ZAYN.
BUT IN THEIR QUEST TO FIND THE LATEST EYE-POPPING
HEADLINES, THEY SOMETIMES TAKE THINGS A LITTLE
TOO FAR. WHILE SOME OF THE STORIES BELOW ARE
BASED ON FACT, OTHERS ARE JUST TALL TALES. CHECK
HOW NEWS SAVVY YOU ARE ON **PAGE 94**.

'ZAYN DOES A RUNNER!'

Zayn has revealed that he will run the London Marathon,
dressed up as Simon Cowell. Zayn has already started
working on his costume and promised to run the 26 miles
in a pair of high-waisted trousers, aviator sunglasses and
a black V-neck T-shirt. He hopes to complete the run in
less than two-and-a-half hours and raise a six-figure sum
for charity.

☐ True News ☐ Fake Fail

'NIGHT OF HIS LIFE'

One Direction claimed that their New York show at Madison
Square Garden on 3rd December 2012, was 'the best night
of their lives'.

☐ True News ☐ Fake Fail

'GET YOUR SKATES ON'

Zayn ended up on crutches after twisting his ankle while skateboarding in LA. Reports suggest that he was staying with Justin Bieber at the time. At LAX airport, cheeky Niall had a huge grin on his face as Zayn hobbled slowly behind.

☐ True News   ☐ Fake Fail

'ZAYN CONKS OUT!'

Zayn has revealed that he has a phobia about conkers. The fear stems from a childhood game of conkers that went horribly wrong. A shard of the shell flew up his nose and had to be removed in hospital.

☐ True News   ☐ Fake Fail

'HEADING FOR A CRASH'

In January 2012 the 1D boys were involved in a minor car accident that gave three of them slight whiplash. Despite the accident, the boys performed at a gig the following night because they didn't want to let down their fans.

☐ True News   ☐ Fake Fail

'WHAT A NUTTER'

Zayn eats a spoonful of crunchy peanut butter before going on stage. He says it helps give his voice a husky quality.

☐ True News   ☐ Fake Fail

Song scramble

ONE DIRECTION'S SONGS ARE ALL SCRAMBLED UP. SEE IF
YOU CAN SORT OUT THE LETTERS BELOW AND UNCOVER
THE SONGS BEHIND THE SCRAMBLE. IF YOU'RE A TRUE
DIRECTIONER, YOU SHOULDN'T HAVE ANY TROUBLE.
CHECK THE ANSWERS ON **PAGE 94** IF YOU GET IN A JAM.

1. LEV WIL YEOG NUHE WIRE

....

2. HONE GINT

....

3. KALS TIRF STISS

....

4. MANT TISH ROHE

....

5. BUT YOG TOEA

....

6. FIBO KAMES HAT LEAW TUUY

....

7. PALL NUG HIT

....

8. YIK SOUS

....

9. TRAT TACK HEA

....

10. TIL GINT HELTS

....

11. NOC NOMMC

....

ARE YOU AN EXPERT WHEN IT COMES TO ZAYN? IT'S
TIME TO PUT YOUR KNOWLEDGE TO THE TEST. TICK THE
BOX NEXT TO EACH FACT THAT YOU ALREADY KNEW
BEFORE YOU STARTED THIS BOOK. THEN TURN TO THE
SUPER-FAN SCORECARD ON **PAGE 90** TO SEE HOW MUCH
OF A ZAYN-BRAINIAC YOU ARE.

☐ Zayn took his English GCSE a year early and, being a
smart fellow, he scored an A.

☐ Harry, Liam and Niall were pranked on Nickelodeon
when an actress, wearing a fake pregnancy bump,
pretended to go into labour just before they were going
to be interviewed. Zayn and Louis were in on the joke
and could barely contain their laughter when the other
lads fell for it.

☐ Zayn almost auditioned for *The X Factor* when he was
15, and then again when he was 16. He finally went
through with it when he was 17, and the rest is history.

☐ When One Direction were voted off in the semi-final of
The X Factor, Zayn told the audience, 'This isn't the end
of One Direction.'

- [ ] Zayn had a bit of a meltdown when it came to performing a group dance routine during *X Factor* boot camp. He hid backstage until Simon Cowell came to find him and convinced him to give it a try.

- [ ] Early in 2012, Zayn deleted his Twitter account, because of the amount of abuse he was receiving. Thankfully, he reinstated it at a later date.

- [ ] Zayn dated his *X Factor* rival Rebecca Ferguson.

- [ ] All the One Direction boys agree that Zayn is the vainest of the group and can't stay away from his own reflection for too long.

- [ ] Zayn claimed that if he had a superpower, he'd like to be able to stay young forever.

- [ ] After being dared to by his cheeky band mates, Zayn once drank a gruesome mixture of mustard, ketchup, Coke and milkshake.

- [ ] If he could swap lives with one of his band mates for the day, Zayn said he'd swap with Louis because he is so hilarious. If he could swap lives with a celebrity, he said it would be David Beckham.

☐ Before appearing on *The X Factor*, Zayn planned to go to university to study English and become a teacher.

☐ Zayn always wears two pairs of socks.

☐ Zayn landed a role in a school production of *Grease* alongside Aqib Khan, who was eventually to star in the film *West is West*.

☐ Outside One Direction, Zayn has two best mates called Danny and Anthony.

SUPER-FAN SCORECARD (A+)

Score 0–5
Must try harder. More commitment is necessary. A tendency for slackness and a lack of concentration.

Score 6–10
Shows promise. Has tried hard and is keen to progress but needs to knuckle down to reach full potential.

Score 11–15
Well done! A fine performance. Has the dedication and enthusiasm to stay at the top of the class.

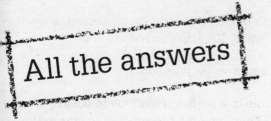
All the answers

Forever young
Pages 6–8

1.	a	**5.**	a	**9.**	c
2.	b	**6.**	a	**10.**	c
3.	a	**7.**	c	**11.**	a
4.	a	**8.**	c	**12.**	a

Super-fans
Pages 16–18

1.	False	**5.**	False	**9.**	False
2.	True	**6.**	False	**10.**	True
3.	True	**7.**	True	**11.**	False
4.	False	**8.**	False	**12.**	False

Favourite things
Pages 19–21

1.	b	**6.**	c	**11.**	a
2.	a	**7.**	a	**12.**	b
3.	a	**8.**	b	**13.**	c
4.	c	**9.**	c		
5.	a	**10.**	b		

True or false?
Pages 22–23

1. True
2. False – It was Niall.
3. True
4. True
5. False – It was Louis.
6. True
7. False – It was Liam.
8. False – It was Harry.
9. True

What was the question?
Pages 26–27

1. J
2. A
3. L
4. D
5. K
6. E

Guess who?
Pages 42–44

1. Louis Tomlinson
2. His mum
3. Harry Styles
4. Robbie Williams
5. Niall Horan
6. Sacha Baron Cohen
7. Liam Payne
8. Michael Jackson
9. His double-jointed thumbs
10. Gucci
11. The 1D tour bus
12. Aeroplane

Cringe!
Pages 46–47

1. False
2. False
3. True
4. True
5. False
6. True
7. True
8. False

Spot the difference (picture section)

1. Zayn has a zip removed from his jacket.
2. Niall's collar is now white.
3. Niall is missing his fourth button.
4. Harry's T-shirt has changed colour.
5. Harry's hanky is missing.
6. Harry's watch is missing.
7. Louis's braces have changed colour.
8. Liam's gun has changed colour.

All directions!
Pages 68–69

Y	T	O	N	E	D	I	R	E	C	T	I	O	N	N
A	A	E	F	I	C	R	M	H	C	O	A	E		O
S	V	I	G	S	H	L	I	R	K	W	S	Y	A	S
H	H	C	M	E	E		M	H	O	S	C	V	L	N
A	A	D	O	L	T	A	I	K	B	H	E	G	L	
P	O	Z	A	Y	N	M	A	L	I	K	M	K	H	L
P	T	F	I	W	P	M	I	O	U	A	C	O		M
E	T	G	K	S	F	A	R	T	M	H	G	G	R	O
N	A	E	S	Y	C	Y	G	R	A	T	R	E	A	T
	T	E	E	R	A	N	C	S	O	K	I	L	N	S
N	A	L	L	R	F	E	D	B	C	F	C	T	H	
M	M	D	T	A	G	T	E	D	E	N	D	A	O	U
W	F	I	I	H	D	B	N	D	H	I	L	A	M	O
T	H	E	X	F	A	C	T	O	R	F	M	B	R	L
V	S	O	N	I	H	T	E	L	T	T	I	L	N	B

Timeline
Pages 80–83

1. 12th January 1993
2. Hair
3. 'Let Me Love You'
4. 'Forever Young'
5. 'What Makes You Beautiful'
6. 19
7. Best British Single
8. April 2012
9. Perrie Edwards
10. Olympics Closing Ceremony
11. Twitter
12. Fastest
13. Justin Bieber
14. *Take Me Home*
15. No. 1
16. Morgan Spurlock

Read all about it!
Pages 84–85

'ZAYN DOES A RUNNER' – Fake Fail

'NIGHT OF HIS LIFE – True News

'GET YOUR SKATES ON' – True News

'ZAYN CONKS OUT' – Fake Fail

'HEADING FOR A CRASH' – True News

'WHAT A NUTTER' – Fake Fail

Song scramble
Pages 86–87

1. 'Live While We're Young'
2. 'One Thing'
3. 'First Last Kiss'
4. 'More Than This'

5. 'Gotta Be You'
6. 'What Makes You Beautiful'
7. 'Up All Night'
8. 'Kiss You'
9. 'Heart Attack'
10. 'Little Things'
11. 'C'mon C'mon'

Also available …

ISBN: 978-1-78055-162-3

ISBN: 978-1-78055-123-4

ISBN: 978-1-78243-013-1